Mi Tierra

written by **Adria Quiñones**
illustrated by **Mrinali Alvarez**

For Winsome
who saw me before I saw myself

Reycraft Books
145 Huguenot Street
New Rochelle, NY 10801

reycraftbooks.com

Reycraft Books is a trade imprint and trademark of Newmark Learning, LLC.

Text © Adria Quiñones

All rights reserved. No portion of this book may be reproduced, stored in a retrieval system, or transmitted in any form or by any means, electronic, mechanical, photocopying, recording, or otherwise, without written permission from the publisher. For information regarding permission, please contact info@reycraftbooks.com.

Educators and Librarians: Our books may be purchased in bulk for promotional, educational, or business use. Please contact sales@reycraftbooks.com.

This is a work of fiction. Names, characters, places, dialogue, and incidents described either are the product of the author's imagination or are used fictitiously. Any resemblance to actual persons, living or dead, is entirely coincidental.

Sale of this book without a front cover or jacket may be unauthorized. If this book is coverless, it may have been reported to the publisher as "unsold or destroyed" and may have deprived the author and publisher of payment.

Library of Congress Control Number: 2024933229

Hardcover ISBN: 978-1-4788-7918-3
Paperback ISBN: 978-1-4788-7919-0

Author photo: Toby Beckwith-Quiñones
Illustrator photo: Courtesy Victor Maldonado

Printed in Dongguan, China. 8557/0624/21312
10 9 8 7 6 5 4 3 2 1

First Edition published by Reycraft Books 2024.

Reycraft Books and Newmark Learning LLC, support diversity and the First Amendment, and celebrate the right to read.

Contents

My Name Is Amaya ... 5

Ñ (Is an Extra Letter) ... 8

Mi Tierra ... 10

Breakfast ... 16

Tía Rosa Wants More Space ... 18

Before It's Night ... 24

Saturday at Tía Rosa's ... 26

My Name Is Amaya

My abuelo named me
after a great Spanish dancer
He said, "She danced
her own way
People thought
only men could dance like that
She had great strength
you may need that
en este pais estraño"

I love that
I don't know
anyone else with my name
there are three Miguels
in my cousin Miguel's class
baby Manuel is Manuelito
so that we don't confuse him
with Tío Manuel
who we call Manolo

Maybe different scares people
they say my name
so many wrong ways
it's simple:

Say Ahhhhhh
like at the doctor's office
remember that sound
and repeat it
two times more
Ah
Ma
Ya

Amaya Ivelisse Nuñez

Ñ *(Is an Extra Letter)*

ñ is an n
with a fancy hat
an n couldn't bear
to be alone
it's an n
holding on
to the sound
of a
y

say
en
yeh

An ñ isn't an uppity n
an n that thinks it's better
than all those other n's
an ñ isn't the n's
long-lost twin
it's a cousin
from far-away
it speaks
with an accent

Ñ
unique
irreplaceable
itself

Sometimes a teacher will say Nunez
is the same as Nuñez but
only one of those is
my name.

Mi Tierra

Every other year
my Abuelo takes a boat or a plane
to come to Washington Heights from Spain.

He walks me to school.
He watches my baby sister.
And he takes us for ice cream.

He cooks dinner
he teaches me the names for food
leche huevos jugo sopa
espaguetis makes me laugh
an Italian name
tossed with Spanish spelling

He stays for 2 or 3 months
until it feels like he'll always
be with us
until I see him start to pack
then I know
we only have a few more days

Why can't you stay with us, Abuelo?
Why do you have to go back to Spain?
"Es mi tierra," he tells me.
"Es mi tierra."

Bronx Grandpa and Grandma
go back to Puerto Rico twice a year
"Por fin," says Grandma when they're
getting ready to leave.
"Regresamos a mi tierra!"

We go to Vermont every summer
every year we stay in the same cabin
every year the same families
every year the same things
swimming in the lake
playing hide-and-seek in the woods
BooBoo from Montreal
Darren from Boston
Izabel and Winnie from Philadelphia

Vermont
is not mi tierra
Vermont needs a car
Washington Heights has subways
Vermont has farms and houses
Washington Heights has parks
and apartment buildings
and a friend who lives
on the other side of your bedroom wall
when you knock they knock
back

Tía Rosa thinks
Washington Heights
has too many people
too close together
she wants a house
and her own backyard
but I like having sidewalks
subway cars to share

When I am old
I will say, "Vamos
a regressar a mi tierra"
just like my grandparents
but it will be Washington Heights

Breakfast

it's the first meal of
the day don't you
want something
healthier more filling
more cereal
eggs
something to
keep you
until lunch
my mom asks
every day
but all I want
is toast

Tía Rosa
Wants More Space

Tía Rosa wants a house
her own yard
"with a fence"

But we have Fort Tryon Park
and Fort Washington Park
by the Hudson River
it's big enough to fit
everyone who wants
to play

"Washington Heights
is too crowded" she says
"you can't raise four boys
in an apartment"
but the boys have bunk beds
with curtains
like four little rooms
one with planets,
one with penguins
one forest, one tie-dyed
it looks so cozy
to me

Tía Rosa and Tío Manolo
live on the 3rd floor
so if we need some milk
we can run downstairs
if Miguelito or Ramón
need help
with homework
they can knock on our door

We see each other
doing laundry
buying groceries
going in and out
every day
Sometimes
when I'm waiting at the window
to see Papi come home
I see Tío Manolo
he looks up and waves

I watch the moving truck
take their things away
I will miss their
hard scratchy couch
the big dining room table
where we did homework
played games
ate Christmas dinner

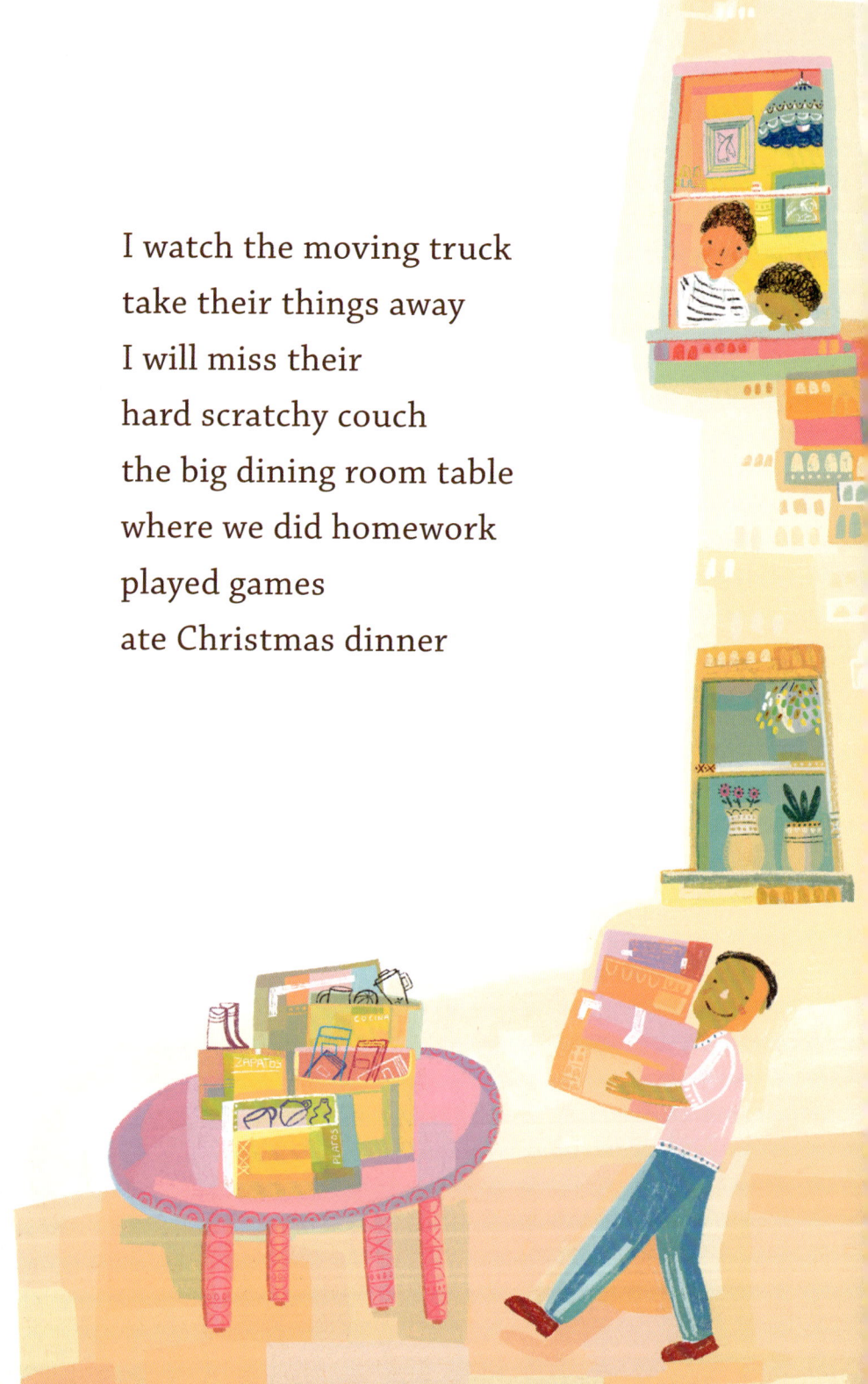

Now we have to make plans
check schedules
maybe Tía Rosa
likes that
too

Before It's Night

The most beautiful time
is right after sunset
the orange-purple-red
clouds fade
to pink and gray
but the sky
holds on
to its blue
hue a little
longer

The street lights
bridge lights
apartment lights
glow gold
For a minute
just for a minute
there are no beeps or honks
just Papi and me
hurrying home
Before it's night

Saturday
at Tía Rosa's

"Come for a barbecue
you can see the house
it's like
a day in the country
good for las niñas
to get out of the city
so much healthier"

We go to Vermont
every summer
I know what
the country is like
Washington Heights has
trees too

"Let me fix your hair,"
my mother says
"And put on
your good shoes"

We used to run to
the third floor
in pajamas
and bare feet
and now I can't
wear sneakers
to see
my cousins

What's so special
about a house?

When we get there
Tía Rosa makes us walk
upstairs
downstairs
showing us everything
that is better
"Wouldn't you like to live
in a nice house like this?"

But there's no bodega
we don't have to cross
the street
to buy milk

If we cross the street
we can get
ramen
sag paneer

mangu con salami
pollo al horno
fried rice
pizza or doughnuts
in the middle of
the night

I say, "No
I like our apartment"
My mother hisses
"No le hables así
 á tu tía
  ¡Que desgracia!"
   Tío laughs
   puts his arm
   around me
   "She's a real
   Nuyorican
   just like me"

He pulls me close
rests his cheek
on my head
as we go outside
to barbecue
on the paved patio
in the yard
surrounded
by a fence

Miguel runs by, hits my arm
and yells, "TAG YOU'RE IT"
I'm about to run
when my mom
puts her hand
on my arm
"Not with your good shoes"
"We have art supplies and stuff"
Ramón suggests
Mom shakes her head
Not in that dress

I can't wait to go home

Adria Quiñones

Adria Quiñones's poetry has appeared in The New York Times. *Amaya Nuñez: Mi Tierra* is her first published work for children and the first part of a trilogy about Amaya, her family, and friends. A lifelong New Yorker, she grew up in Queens and now lives in Washington Heights, where she likes to watch the tugs on the Hudson and the traffic on the George Washington Bridge.

Mrinali Alvarez

Mrinali Alvarez Astacio is a Puerto Rican illustrator and author. The Carnegie Mellon Foundation and Fundación Flamboyán granted her the Letras Boricuas scholarship in 2021. Mrinali holds an MA and a PhD in Children's Book Illustration from the Cambridge School of Art at Anglia Ruskin University in the United Kingdom.